NATURE HEALS

CAMPING IN NATURE

BY ABBY COLICH

BLUE OWL BOOKS

TIPS FOR CAREGIVERS

Social and emotional learning (SEL) helps children manage emotions, learn how to feel empathy, create and achieve goals, and make good decisions. One goal of teaching SEL skills is to help children care for themselves, others, and the world around them. The more time children spend in nature and the more they learn about it, the more likely they will be to appreciate it and receive its emotional benefits.

BEFORE READING

Talk to the reader about ways to spend time outdoors. Talk about how camping is one way he or she can spend more time in nature.

Discuss: What are things you like to do outside? Have you ever been camping? If so, what kinds of activities did you do while you were camping?

AFTER READING

Talk to the reader about what it means to feel more connected to nature.

Discuss: How do you feel after you do an activity outside? Do you feel differently after you've spent time in nature?

SEL GOAL

Children may struggle with processing their emotions, and they may lack accessible tools to help them do so. Explain to children that nature can help people feel good. Doing activities in nature, like camping, can help children learn new skills and how to work with others. Encourage children to find a way to feel more connected to nature, even if they can't go camping. Sitting outside and practicing deep breathing techniques or focusing on all five senses are great activities to help bring a child closer to nature.

TABLE OF CONTENTS

CHAPTER 1

MINDFUL CAMPING

Have you ever been camping? Camping allows you to do many things that are different from your everyday life. You sleep outside. You make food around a fire. Did you know camping can be good for you, too?

Spending time in nature can help you be more **mindful**. It helps you relax and **focus** on what is happening in the moment. When you go camping, you get to learn and experience new things. It can help you learn to be **resourceful**.

Prepare for your camping trip by planning when and where you will go. Then pack the supplies you'll need, such as a tent, food, and a sleeping bag. Check the forecast. Make sure you have the right clothing for the weather.

PACK LIGHT

Only pack what you will need. Living with less for a few days makes it easier to connect with nature. Leave your **devices** at home or try not to use them. Let the quiet outside help quiet your mind.

If you can't go camping, that is OK! Ask a parent or guardian if you can sleep in a tent in your yard for a night. Or build a tent indoors. Use a sheet or blanket. Close your eyes. Think about a scene from nature. Slowly breathe in and out for a few minutes. Then open your eyes. Do you feel calmer?

CHAPTER 2

TIME TO CAMP!

When you go camping, you get to spend a lot of time outside. Focus on the nature you can't see at home. What **scenery** is around you? You may see woods, mountains, or bodies of water. Breathe in the fresh air.

Observe plants and animals. Do you hear birds, bugs, or other sounds? How does this experience in nature make you feel?

Camping teaches you skills. Learning new skills teaches you **perseverance**. Putting a tent up isn't easy. You may not get it the first time, but keep trying. When you finally get it right, you will feel proud.

Camping can involve other activities. Try going on a hike. If you are near water, go swimming or fishing. These can be great exercise. Or if you just feel like relaxing, that's OK, too!

CHAPTER 3

CAMPING AND TEAMWORK

Camping is a great way to spend time with others. It takes **teamwork**. You will need to **communicate**. Talk about who will do jobs, such as setting up the campsite, getting water, cooking, and cleaning dishes. Be **patient** with others as they learn new things.

Play games or go on a scavenger hunt to have fun with others on your trip. What activities can you think of that allow you to spend time with others?

A campfire can help you cook food and keep warm. It provides light, too. An adult can show you how to safely start a fire and keep it controlled. Sitting around a fire is a great way to spend time with others. You might sing or tell stories. What do you want to talk about?

WATCHING THE FIRE

Listen to the wood crackle as it burns. How does the smoke smell? Look for different colors in the flames. Picture your worries or **negative** thoughts burning in the flames.

Camping can help you reset. Your mind may feel clearer. You may have more **energy** or feel more **creative**. Camping can be hard work, but it can help you build perseverance. Take time to feel proud of all you **achieved**.

CARE FOR YOUR CAMPSITE

Be mindful of your campsite and nature. Throw your trash away. Don't feed animals or remove plants. Take your things with you when you leave.

GOALS AND TOOLS

GROW WITH GOALS

Camping is one way you can feel more connected to nature.

Goal: Keep a camping journal. Write about what you saw, did, learned, and felt while you were camping.

Goal: After camping, make a list of all the things you liked or appreciated about being in nature.

Goal: Take a break! Even if you can't go camping, go outside for 20 minutes. Be mindful of any wildlife around you. Do you feel better when you go back inside?

MINDFULNESS EXERCISE

Picture a spot that you have been to in nature and that you enjoy. Or picture a spot you would like to visit. Sit up straight and tall. Close your eyes. Slowly breathe in and out. Imagine yourself in that space. What do you see around you? What noises do you hear? What do you smell? How does your body feel? Keep your mind in this place for a few minutes. Then open your eyes. Do you feel differently now?

GLOSSARY

achieved
Did something successfully after making an effort.

communicate
To share information, ideas, or feelings with another person through language, eye contact, or gestures.

creative
Skillful at using your imagination and thinking of new ideas.

devices
Pieces of equipment with computers inside, such as smartphones or tablets.

energy
The ability or strength to do things without getting tired.

focus
To concentrate on something.

mindful
A mentality achieved by focusing on the present moment and calmly recognizing and accepting your feelings, thoughts, and sensations.

negative
Focusing on the bad side of a situation, person, or thing.

observe
To watch someone or something closely, especially to learn something.

patient
Able to put up with problems or delays without getting angry or upset.

perseverance
The act of continuing to do or try something, even if you have difficulties.

resourceful
Able to deal with and find clever solutions to problems.

scenery
Outdoor scenes or views that are pleasing to look at.

teamwork
The work done by a group of people who accomplish something together.

TO LEARN MORE

FACT SURFER

Finding more information is as easy as 1, 2, 3.

1. Go to www.factsurfer.com
2. Enter "**campinginnature**" into the search box.
3. Choose your book to see a list of websites.

INDEX

Blue Owl Books are published by Jump!, 5357 Penn Avenue South, Minneapolis, MN 55419, www.jumplibrary.com

Library of Congress Cataloging-in-Publication Data

Names: Colich, Abby, author.
Title: Camping in nature / by Abby Colich.
Description: Minneapolis: Jump!, Inc., 2021.
Series: Nature heals | Includes index. | Audience: Ages 7–10
Identifiers: LCCN 2020039569 (print)
LCCN 2020039570 (ebook)
ISBN 9781645278283 (hardcover)
ISBN 9781645278290 (paperback)
ISBN 9781645278306 (ebook)
Subjects: LCSH: Camping–Juvenile literature. | Nature–Juvenile literature. | Mindfulness (Psychology)–Juvenile literature.
Classification: LCC GV191.7 .C65 2021 (print) | LCC GV191.7 (ebook) | DDC 796.54–dc23
LC record available at https://lccn.loc.gov/2020039569
LC ebook record available at https://lccn.loc.gov/2020039570

Editor: Eliza Leahy
Designer: Michelle Sonnek

Photo Credits: simoly/Shutterstock, cover; New Africa/Shutterstock, 1, 3, 6–7; Rawpixel.com/Shutterstock, 4; PeopleImages/iStock, 5; kryzhov/Shutterstock, 8–9; Africa Studio/Shutterstock, 10; jarabee123/Shutterstock, 11; Roman Pelesh/Shutterstock, 12–13; Monkey Business Images/Shutterstock, 14–15; Warut Chinsai/Shutterstock, 16 (left); wavebreakmedia/Shutterstock, 16 (right), 17; milkjko/iStock, 18–19; Sergey Novikov/Shutterstock, 20–21.

Printed in the United States of America at Corporate Graphics in North Mankato, Minnesota.